Sir Gadabout
Does His Best

Also by Martyn Beardsley

Sir Gadabout
Sir Gadabout Gets Worse
Sir Gadabout and the Ghost
Sir Gadabout Goes Barking Mad

Find out more about **Sir Gadabout** at
http://mysite.wanadoo-members.co.uk/gadabout

Also by Martyn Beardsley

Sir Gadabout

When the fair Guinevere goes missing, Sir Gadabout sets out on a quest to rescue her ... and he's in for some catastrophic adventures!

Sir Gadabout Gets Worse

When Excalibur is stolen, Gads sets off with his trusty band of followers to find the evil Sir Rudyard the Rancid. They must face the worst if they are to return the mighty sword to its rightful home.

Sir Gadabout and The Ghost

When he sees the ghost of Sir Henry Hirsute, Gads runs up the wall in fright. But soon he's off on another calamitous quest – to clear Sir Henry's name of the ghastly crime of pilchard-stealing.

Martyn Beardsley

Sir Gadabout

Does His Best

Illustrated by Tony Ross

Orion
Children's Books

First published in Great Britain in 2001
as a Dolphin Paperback
Reissued in 2006 by Orion Children's Books
a division of the Orion Publishing Group Ltd
Orion House
5 Upper St Martin's Lane
London WC2H 9EA

1 3 5 7 9 10 8 6 4 2

A catalogue record for this book
is available from the British Library

Printed in Great Britain by Clays Ltd, St Ives plc

ISBN-13 978 1 85881 892 4
ISBN-10 1 85881 892 3

The Orion Publishing Group's policy is to use papers that are natural,
renewable and recyclable products and made from wood grown in sustainable
forests. The logging and manufacturing processes are expected to conform to
the environmental regulations of the country of origin.

www.orionbooks.co.uk

Contents

1   The Knights of
    the Green Cross   1

2   The Contest   13

3   The First Clue   36

4   Hot Work   53

5   The Circus   70

1

The Knights of the Green Cross

A long, long time ago, even before anyone had managed to collect a full set of Pokémon cards, there was a castle called Camelot. You couldn't miss it – it had massive walls and towers so tall they had snow on top even in the summer.

Once upon a time King Arthur lived at Camelot. He was a great warrior and one of the most famous kings of all time, although he did suffer a lot from nosebleeds. Despite what some people said, these were *never* caused by picking, though he did sometimes *scratch* his nose, which is completely different as you know.

Arthur's queen was called Guinevere. She was so beautiful that all the knights had posters of her on their walls; and she was so good at woodwork that there was always a queue of people outside her door with broken tables and chairs, and those bookcases that you have to put together yourself and always end up with one piece left over that should have gone in at the beginning.

King Arthur was in charge of the Knights of the Round Table, which had been made by Guinevere with a special saw he had given her one Christmas. They were the greatest knights in the land – well, all except one. His name was Sir Gadabout. He wasn't *quite* as good as the others. One day, thinking he was charging at an evil knight, he had given a rhubarb seller on horseback a *terrible* fright. And the rhubarb seller *won*. Sir Gadabout ended up having to have a stick of rhubarb removed *very* carefully from up his nose by Merlin the wizard.

He was so bad that mothers would frighten their children by saying they would end up like Sir Gadabout if they were naughty.

Sir Gadabout was the Worst Knight in the World. Or at least that's what everyone in Camelot thought. But then something happened that made the knights of Camelot wonder if there might just be someone who was *worse*.

A messenger hurried to King Arthur's side while everyone was in Camelot's great hall at a banquet in honour of Sir Dorothy (some of the knights had *very* unusual names), who was getting married (to a lady called Dorothy, funnily enough).

The king rose. "May I have your attention. We have unexpected visitors, and though we are in the middle of congratulating one of our finest knights, I hope we shall all show them a warm Camelot welcome."

As soon as he had finished speaking, a small group of knights entered the hall carrying a

white banner bearing a green cross.

"I am Sir Melville, lord of the Knights of the Green Cross. We come from the fine town of Milton Keynes, a place where the ladies are fair and the men are fairly brave."

"Welcome, Sir Melville," said King Arthur. "A toast to our visitors!" And so saying, he and Guinevere banged their tankards together and everyone else joined in. There was a loud crash. They looked round and saw a knight holding the handle of a smashed tankard in his hand.

"My clothes are all *wet*," he groaned.

"Sir Gadabout?" asked Sir Melville.

"Indeed," replied King Arthur. "Have you heard of him?"

"His fame has spread far and wide. In fact, that brings me to the reason for our visit. May we talk in private?"

The following morning, King Arthur sent for Herbert, Sir Gadabout's loyal squire and helper. Herbert was short and stocky and packed a powerful punch. If you ever say anything nasty about Sir Gadabout, don't do it when Herbert's around! But on this occasion he was feeling rather nervous. Not being a knight, Herbert never usually went to see the king alone, so he was worried in case he had done something wrong.

The king wanted to see Herbert about a very important plan concerning Sir Gadabout but Herbert wondered if it was something to do with the bubble gum wrapper he had thrown behind King Arthur's throne when no one was looking.

The more he thought about it, the more he became convinced that he had been found

out. The bubble gum wrapper grew larger and dirtier in his imagination. It grew as large as a tablecloth. What if Corky, the queen's favourite cat had crept under it and suffocated?

Solemnly, Herbert approached the royal thrones as the king and queen regally watched him. They were smiling cheerfully but since he felt too guilty even to look at them, he imagined they were scowling and snarling. In his mind the bubble gum wrapper was now the size of a bed sheet. Corky would *never* be able to get out! Herbert could contain himself no longer; he ran the last few metres, throwing himself sobbing at Guinevere's feet.

"I never *meant* to kill the cat, Your Majesty! It was sheer laziness! I deserve to be *hanged*!" Then, realising what he'd just said, added meekly, "Or perhaps put in the stocks."

Arthur and Guinevere looked at each other, scratching their heads (their own heads, not each other's) and wearing very puzzled expressions.

Now on his knees, Herbert, through his tears, had a good view of behind Arthur's throne. He could see Corky, the queen's favourite cat. He could see Corky contentedly licking a red and yellow bubble gum wrapper. He could see that it was a *very small* bubble gum wrapper.

Slowly, Herbert picked himself up, wiped his eyes, and dusted himself down. "Er, you wanted to see me, Your Majesty?" he enquired casually.

"Are you quite all right?" the king asked.

"If you're not feeling well——" Guinevere began.

"Just a bit of a cold," fibbed Herbert. "I was, er, just sneezing." He did a sneeze, trying to make it sound at least a *little* bit like "*never meant to kill the cat . . .*" but it came out much less convincingly than he'd imagined.

Guinevere looked horrified. Arthur went pale. "I'm sending for the Royal Physician immediately," he said.

Herbert finally managed to convince them that he was neither ill nor mad. They put it down to spending so much time with Sir Gadabout, which led the king on to why he had sent for Herbert in the first place.

"This is a very delicate matter, Herbert," King Arthur explained. "You see, the Knights of the Green Cross believe they have a knight who is worse than Sir Gadabout! His name is

Sir Mistabit. Apparently he got his name from his previous job as a painter and decorator. They say he has caused accidents involving twenty-eight people and one goat this year alone."

"The king and I have never wanted to believe that our Gads is the worst knight in the world," said Guinevere. "Now we can prove it! There is to be a contest between Sir Gadabout and Sir Mistabit to settle the matter."

"Oh..." said Herbert thoughtfully. He *certainly* never thought his master was the worst knight in the world. Now there would be a chance for justice!

"However," added Arthur, "since I... I mean we... I mean..."

"*I* have decided that it would be too cruel to tell Gads that the contest is to see who is the worst knight in the world," declared Guinevere. "I was wondering if you would help us by telling a harmless little white lie?"

"We want him to think," continued Arthur, "that it's a contest to decide who is Knight of the Year. It's a competition they have in *Knight's Monthly* magazine. Have you ever read

it? It's very good! Last month they had free glitter stickers on the cover with shapes of castles and horses and so on. I stuck some on my armour, but Guinevere—"

"As the king was saying," interrupted Guinevere, "we would like to know if you will persuade him that it's a contest for Knight of the Year, just to save his feelings."

"I'm not sure," Herbert faltered. "I don't like telling—" At that moment Corky emerged from behind the throne with a red and yellow bubble gum wrapper in his mouth.

"Oh, all right then."

2

The Contest

"*Knight's Monthly!*" cried Sir Gadabout excitedly. "My favourite magazine! I've still got my free *Knight's Notebook*. I write all my important numbers in it."

"What sort of numbers?" asked Sidney Smith. He was Merlin the wizard's ginger and very sarcastic cat who happened to be paying a visit. He had helped them on many of their quests (being quite clever, *and* having picked up some of Merlin's magic). Whenever he was bored, he tended to hang around Sir Gadabout for a laugh.

"Well, er, six... and eight, my lucky number, and ten's quite important because it's a decimal... I think."

"Never mind the *Knight's Notebook*," said Herbert, who always got nervous about anything involving numbers. "We've got to get

ready for the contest."

"I might win! I've always wanted to be on the front cover of *Knight's Monthly*!" babbled Sir Gadabout, getting even more excited.

"You already have been," Sidney Smith pointed out. "Remember the time you set fire to the King of Gaul's moustache?"

"That doesn't count," said Herbert sharply.

"It was an *accident*!" protested Sir Gadabout. "Anyway, do you think they'll be sending a reporter – to interview me and everything?"

"Definitely." Herbert started to worry about how good a liar he was becoming. "We're expected on the fields outside Camelot in five minutes. Time to go, Sire."

"This ought to be good fun," sniggered Sidney Smith.

Herbert helped Sir Gadabout into his armour. His old armour had completely fallen to bits and this was his first chance to wear his brand new set.

"I dare say I'll be able to buy some *proper* armour if I win the money," said Sir Gadabout dreamily. "There is a cash prize?"

"Whopping big one, Sire," fibbed Herbert. Well, it wouldn't be *his* problem to sort out.

"I want to get something with three stripes down the arms, or a sort of tick on the helmet – you know, like Sir Lancelot."

The problem with Sir Gadabout's new armour was that it was made of cardboard. It had come free with August's *Knight's Monthly*. It wasn't actually meant to be worn but Sir Gadabout thought it was pretty *tough* cardboard and as usual he was rather broke.

"Very smart helmet, Sire," Herbert remarked as he helped his master put it on. He had painted it (and the rest of the armour) an

impressive deep blue with his own water-colours (free with last week's *Today's Squire*).

"Do you think it would withstand a blow from a sword?" Sir Gadabout asked.

Sidney Smith guffawed. "That thing wouldn't withstand a blow from a penny whistle!"

"Hmm," said Herbert, giving the helmet a sharp tap with his hand. One of his fingers went straight through the cardboard.

"Oww!" cried Sir Gadabout. "Your finger is in my eye!"

"So sorry, Sire. Allow me to remove it," said Herbert helpfully. He pulled his finger out, leaving a small hole in the helmet.

"Better hope Sir Mistabit's got a cardboard sword," said Sidney Smith with a catty snigger.

Sir Gadabout gulped.

Sir Gadabout marched into the middle of the field, followed by Herbert leading Sir Gadabout's new horse. His old horse Pegasus was in well-earned retirement after he'd finally had a nervous breakdown towards the end of their last adventure. Herbert had bought a new steed at a bargain price from Honest Alf of Diddlem, a village not far from Camelot. The horse, Buck, had been rescued from a travelling show in which he had been cruelly used by a stuntman for death-defying jumps over fire, snakes, and other terrifying things. Herbert had taken pity on Buck. Unlike Pegasus, he was young, lean and fast, and Herbert had soon learned not to say *Jump!* within his earshot. Buck *really* didn't like that word.

What Sir Gadabout didn't know, as he strode boldly forward to meet Sir Mistabit, was that his opponent was not a tall man. In

fact, he was *tiny*. When Sir Gadabout came across a very small person in armour — who reached just about up to his own knees — he said, "Run along, now, little boy. A *very* important contest is about to take place."

Sir Mistabit kicked Sir Gadabout on the shin.

"OUCH! I won't tell you again — go and

play at knights with the other boys!"

"Who are you calling a boy?" Sir Mistabit demanded, giving Sir Gadabout another kick.

"OOYAH! You've got children's armour on. And stop *kicking!*"

"*You've* got children's armour on," said Sir Mistabit, poking his finger through the cardboard around Sir Gadabout's knee and

making another hole in the armour.

Sir Gadabout retaliated by lifting Sir Mistabit up in the air and giving him a good rattle.

The crowd, who had been getting fed up with waiting, were beginning to enjoy themselves.

"Did you make that outfit using 'Origarmour', Gads?"

"Bite his ankles, Tiny!"

Sir Gadabout and Sir Mistabit ended up rolling around on the ground in a very untidy scuffle, flapping and tweaking and calling each other names, and making the crowd roar with laughter. Finally, Sir Mistabit pretended to give in and walk away, but suddenly he turned sharply and ran full pelt at Sir Gadabout with his head down to butt him like a goat. Sir Gadabout tended to freeze like a statue when he was taken by surprise. He stood, his feet rooted to the spot and his mouth hanging open as Sir Mistabit rushed towards him.

Just as the crowd expected an almighty collision, Sir Mistabit charged right through Sir Gadabout's trembling legs, under a table with some drinks on it, and finally rammed his helmet against the bottom of a three-legged

goat which had been happily munching grass.

"*Ooooh!*" cried the crowd, who quite liked goats.

Lucky the goat wasn't just any goat. She was a Pyrenean mountain goat and the mascot of the Knights of the Green Cross. Sadly, Lucky only had three legs. She used to have four but that was before she met Sir Mistabit.

The poor creature gave a startled bleat and

galloped away. Sir Mistabit sat on the grass in a daze.

"Serves him right, trying to cheat like that!" said Herbert, joining his master.

"Who was he?" asked Sir Gadabout.

"Didn't you know? That was Sir Mistabit!"

"But—" began Sir Gadabout.

He was distracted by a noise from the crowd. They were all looking at a scoreboard at the end of the field. It said:

| Sir Mistabit | 1 | Sir Gadabout | ⊙ |

Sidney Smith groaned.

Herbert cheered.

Sir Gadabout didn't understand. "But, but, if we're trying to find the Knight of the Year, and he just missed me and bumped into a three-legged goat, how come—"

"Never mind, Sire. Keep it up!" said Herbert, patting him on the back and making another hole in the armour.

The next contest was a joust. The knights, each holding a long lance, had to charge at one another on horseback and try to knock the other off.

All was going well. Sir Mistabit had mounted his horse with the aid of a ladder. He had three gingham cushions on his saddle so that he could see over the horse's head. Sir Gadabout was sitting on Buck, quite excited at the prospect of charging on such a fast young animal. But just as they were about to begin, things took an unexpected turn.

Sidney Smith had been skulking around the rear of Sir Gadabout's horse. He had bet quite a bit of money on Sir Gadabout *still* being the Worst Knight in the World, and thought he knew a way to make it happen. Herbert asked him what he was up to.

"I'm just here to give him some encouragement," replied the cat slyly.

"Hmm," said Herbert, unconvinced. But the time had come.

"Right – off you go, Sire!"

"Yes!" shouted Sidney Smith. "JUMP to it!"

Buck heard the word *jump*, gave a loud neigh and shot off – but not in the direction that Sir Gadabout wanted him to go. The horse felt sure there would be snakes or leaping flames somewhere in *that* direction. He galloped wild-eyed around the field looking for an exit. Sir Gadabout, who wasn't used to such speed, was bouncing around in the saddle, holding grimly onto the reins. To make matters worse, it had started to rain quite heavily. It was hard to see and the wet reins kept slipping through his hands.

Sir Mistabit set off in hot pursuit. "Come back, coward! Call me a little boy, would you? You can't run forever!"

Buck, too, realised he couldn't run forever and, unable to find a way out through the crowd, he decided he must get rid of his rider. It was just like a Wild West rodeo. Buck jumped and kicked and twisted and turned, all so violently that it seemed Sir Gadabout *must* be thrown off. But the crowd cheered wildly when it looked, amazingly, as though Sir Gadabout was going to hang on. They had never thought of Gads as being a fantastic horseman. What they didn't know was that the reins, what with all the slipping and grabbing, had now become entangled around his arm. He was stuck!

The judges had never seen such horsemanship. Sir Mistabit simply couldn't catch him. It was beginning to look like 2–0.

By now, Sir Mistabit had stopped chasing and had made himself room for one last charge. Buck was jumping and kicking on the spot, trying like mad to get rid of Sir Gadabout. The horse couldn't understand it. No one had ever lasted this long.

Sir Mistabit saw his opportunity. He levelled his lance, dug his spurs in, and . . . *charged*!

The rain had completely soaked Sir Gadabout's cardboard armour and there was now very little of it left. His cardboard breastplate had turned into a soggy pulp and oozed down into his lap, where it looked rather like a nappy. As Sir Mistabit hurtled along pointing his long lance, Sir Gadabout sat shivering in the saddle in his string vest.

The ground began to shake as Sir Mistabit, one hand clutching his deadly lance, the other clinging gamely to his gingham cushions, flew right at Sir Gadabout.

Sir Gadabout was desperately trying to get his hand free from the reins. At the very last second, just as he saw the wickedly sharp point of Sir Mistabit's lance coming right for

his nose, Sir Gadabout did it.

His hand came free. Buck bucked and Sir Gadabout shot skyward.

Sir Mistabit's lance pierced only fresh air as he whizzed past.

"*Whaaaat?*" he roared. Everything had happened too quickly for him to see what had become of Sir Gadabout. He didn't have to wait long because Sir Gadabout landed right on top of him.

The joust ended with Sir Mistabit riding around the field flailing his arms about in vain at Sir Gadabout, who was sitting on the little knight's shoulders, clinging to his head and wearing only a string vest and a cardboard nappy.

The crowd were laughing so much it gave them all tummy aches, and the scoreboard said:

Sir Mistabit	1	Sir Gadabout	1

"That's more like the Sir Gadabout we know and love!" purred Sidney Smith.

"Just you wait till this is over," growled Herbert.

He was about to try getting Sir Gadabout ready for the next contest, when King Arthur and Sir Melville, the head of the Knights of the Green Cross, hurried towards them looking worried.

"The competition must be halted," cried King Arthur.

"*Awww!*" shouted the crowd, who hadn't had so much fun in ages.

"But— I can get him some more armour in a jiffy, Your Majesty!" Herbert said. "I know his vest's not as clean as it might be but *some* of that is blue paint from—"

"It's not that," said Sir Melville. "It's Lucky the goat. She's our mascot and is extremely important to the Knights of the Green Cross."

"Lucky has run away and she must be found," added King Arthur gravely. "All of our knights will search until she's brought back safely."

"*All* of them?" queried Sidney Smith, gazing at Sir Gadabout and Sir Mistabit who were still galloping around like a circus act.

They were arguing furiously. Sir Gadabout was pulling Sir Mistabit's ears and Sir Mistabit kept biting Sir Gadabout's knees.

"*OUCH*! Stop it!"

"*Arggh*! You started it!"

"All of them," sighed the king.

3

The First Clue

"We must act quickly if we are to save Lucky," said King Arthur to Sir Gadabout and Sir Mistabit.

All the other knights had already gone out searching but these two needed, well, a bit of extra advice.

"We've had reports of more dragons than usual being on the prowl. We've got to find Lucky before they do," the king added.

"There are lots of goats in the countryside around here, Your Majesty," said Sir Gadabout. "How will we recognise her?"

"The three legs will give you a clue," remarked Sidney Smith.

"How did she lose her leg?" asked Herbert.

"Sir Mistabit was bringing Lucky to our castle and she was run over by a hay cart, sadly," replied Sir Melville.

"A very *fast* hay cart," added Sir Mistabit.

"I see . . . I think," said the king. "But time is precious. Sir Gadabout knows the area, so Sir Mistabit will accompany him."

"Begging your pardon, Majesty, but I don't need that overgrown ear-puller to show me the way," said Sir Mistabit haughtily.

Sir Gadabout walked up to the tiny knight – well, it was more of a waddle, really. Now that the sun was out, his squelchy cardboard "nappy" had hardened into a sort of *papier-mâché* plaster cast – the sort that is put on a broken leg. It certainly made getting about extremely difficult. "You're a little rude, aren't you?"

"I'm not LITTLE!" yelled Sir Mistabit.

"Of course not. It's just that everyone else is very big," Sidney Smith commented.

"Enough of this bickering!" cried Sir Melville. "I don't think you people at Camelot realise just how important Lucky is to us. You *must* get her back safe and sound!"

"We shall do our best," promised King Arthur. And he sent Sir Gadabout and Sir Mistabit on their way immediately.

The only path that had not been taken by any of the other knights was the road to

Upper Gumtrey, so off they went: Sir Gadabout riding Buck with Herbert and Sidney
Smith in tow, and Sir Mistabit on his own
horse.

They rode down a very long, pleasant, leafy
lane, until they came to a narrow path leading
off to the right with a sign saying:

PRIVATE PROPERTY – KEEP OUT.

The sign reads: "Private Property KEEP OUT"

"I wonder who lives down there?" mused Sir Gadabout.

"Maybe they've seen Lucky. We ought to check," said Sir Mistabit.

"That's Ma Rockall's cottage," said Sidney Smith. "She's Merlin's cleaning lady."

"But Merlin's house is all dark and dusty," said Herbert.

"She's a very *tough* woman," the ginger cat

explained. "Merlin once complained about a cobweb she'd missed and she was so mad she shoved him up the chimney and started a fire. He doesn't send for her much these days."

"Didn't he cast a spell on her?" Sir Gadabout asked.

"She grabbed his magic wand and ate it before his eyes," Sidney Smith said, shuddering at the memory.

"Er, she probably won't know anything about Lucky," said Sir Gadabout, turning away from the path. "In fact, *definitely* probably."

He was so keen to get going he was almost prepared to shout "*Jump!*" and hold on to Buck for dear life.

But Sir Mistabit was having none of it. He trotted down Ma Rockall's path. "I am a Knight of the Green Cross, fearless and strong and of almost average height!" he declared.

"Average for a guinea pig, maybe," muttered Sidney Smith.

"Well, er, it's possibly worth checking—' Sir Gadabout faltered.

"No *possibly* about it!" cried Sir Mistabit. "The Knights of the Green Cross— What on earth's *that?*"

Heading towards them at incredible speed

was a turtle riding a black and white rabbit. The turtle was holding a barbecue skewer like a lance, wore a teacup for a helmet, and carried a saucer as a shield with **McP** daubed on it in bright red.

"I forgot," sighed Sidney Smith. "Dr McPherson takes his holidays with Ma Rockall. She used to polish his shell and they became firm friends. And now he gets all his best ideas from her."

Dr McPherson was Merlin's guard-turtle. He attacked anyone who visited the magician, even Sidney, thinking he was defending his master's property. He had some *interesting* ideas on how to surprise people, to say the least — but none that seemed to work.

Sir Mistabit simply moved his horse to one side and Dr McPherson whizzed straight past on his rabbit. The rabbit had never been let out of his hutch before and wasn't going to miss this chance to join his friends in the countryside.

"Stop!" cried Sidney Smith.

"I *caaaaaaaaan't!*" Dr McPherson's voice faded away as the rabbit fled across the road and over a hill to freedom.

"Very dangerous, running across the road like that without looking," commented Sir Mistabit.

"I bet that's what Lucky thought when she counted her legs and found there were only three," replied Sidney Smith.

"The hay cart was not equipped with a hooter," Sir Mistabit responded angrily.

Eventually, they proceeded along the winding path to Ma Rockall's cottage. Every garment hanging on her washing line was full of ragged holes.

"That's funny," said Sidney Smith. "Ma

Rockall's usually *very* fussy about her things being in perfect condition."

Sir Gadabout knocked on the door. It was opened by a short (not as short as Sir Mistabit) but extremely solid woman with arms like sides of beef and a face like thunder.

"Say what you want and quick about it," she boomed. "Got work to do. Wish *I* had time to go knocking on people's doors!"

"Er, have you seen a goat?" asked Sir Gadabout.

"GOAT?" exclaimed Ma Rockall in a voice that sounded like a volcano erupting.

She grabbed Sir Gadabout by the scruff of the neck and dragged him, clanking (Guinevere had knocked him up a new suit of armour out of baked bean tins) to the washing line. "I'll give him GOAT!"

She snatched a holey apron from the line. "What do you think did *this*?"

"A very large moth?" ventured Sir Gadabout.

The others winced as Ma Rockall's face darkened.

"*Moth*, eh?" she said as she stuffed the apron down the back of his neck.

"P-perhaps a s-sort of caterpillar—"

"I'll give him *caterpillar*," she growled as she rammed various ruined garments from the washing line (some of them very private and personal) into any available gap or crevice in Sir Gadabout's armour.

"Try '*goat*', Sire," whispered Herbert.

Sir Gadabout said, "*Gmmpmph* . . ." Then he coughed something with frills and elastic out of his mouth and repeated meekly, "Goat?"

"Oh – GOAT he thinks, does he?"

She took a fistful of one of Sir Gadabout's ears and dragged him like a rag doll into the cottage. The others followed at a safe distance.

The inside of the cottage was a complete mess. Chair and table legs had been chewed, wallpaper had been torn and half eaten in several places; even the carpet had holes.

"I suppose a *very large mouse* did all this monstrousness?" she asked, glaring at him.

All of Sir Gadabout's different-sized tin cans were rattling together and playing a little tune (rather like *London Bridge is Falling Down*).

It was clear that Lucky had been here

before them – but the only way they could get Ma Rockall to give them any details was to tidy the cottage *and* put up new wallpaper for her.

Herbert and Sidney Smith got busy in the kitchen while Sir Gadabout and Sir Mistabit wallpapered the living room. At least, they *tried* to. Sir Gadabout did the pasting and Sir Mistabit stood on a stepladder to stick the paper up – but he couldn't reach the top of the wall. So, Sir Mistabit did the pasting – but he was too short to pass the paper up to Sir Gadabout at the top of the steps, and so it went on.

There was more wallpaper stuck to Sir Gadabout's armour than to the walls, and when Sir Mistabit slipped on some paste and knocked over the stepladder, sending Sir Gadabout flying into Ma Rockall's mighty arms, enough was enough.

"STOP! STOP! STOP!" she bellowed into Sir Gadabout's ear as she held him in her arms like a baby. "I'll tell you about the blinking goat if you'll just get out of my cottage before it falls down around my ears!"

"If you will kindly let me go, madam," suggested Sir Gadabout.

She did — very quickly. He hit the floor with a great CLANGING and groaning.

"The little varmint scarpered about an hour ago," growled Ma Rockall.

"Are you sure it was *our* goat? Did it have three legs?"

"Nope."

"Then you've been wasting our time!" complained Sir Mistabit.

Ma Rockall glared at him so fiercely that steam came out of her ears. "If you don't teach your son some manners," she said to Sir Gadabout, "*I'll* waste his time all right . . ." and she rolled her sleeves up even higher — as far as her muscles would allow.

"*Son!*" chortled Sidney Smith.

Ma Rockall gave *him* such a look that his whiskers wilted and he slunk behind Herbert and kept quiet.

"Our goat has three legs," Sir Gadabout explained.

Ma Rockall went into her kitchen and opened the fridge door. "The little cottage-wrecker jumped onto the table to get at some food. My carving knife was on the table — and it's *very* sharp . . ." She pulled from the fridge what looked very much like a goat's leg.

"DINNER!" she cried.

"Now Lucky's only got *two* legs!" said Herbert. "Which way did she go?"

"She went over Clay Hill and headed north."

"B-but that's towards the *Dragon Zone!*" gasped Sir Gadabout.

"Forward!" cried Sir Mistabit, marching to the door.

"B-but *fire*... and *claws*... and great big—"

"Scared?" asked Sir Mistabit, already outside.

"No, he's not!" answered Herbert, gently pushing his trembling master out.

"We're all dead men," muttered Sidney Smith as he followed them to the wildest and most dangerous place in the whole country.

4

Hot Work

The Dragon Zone was cold and bleak and stretched for miles and miles. Nobody (except dragons) lived there. One moment it could be clear, the next you could be engulfed in thick fog and completely lost. Or you might step into a treacherous bog from which it was almost impossible to escape. There were strange noises, like whimpering and teeth chattering – but since these came from Sir Gadabout perhaps they didn't count.

As if all that wasn't bad enough, around every corner there was the chance that they would encounter a *dragon*. Dragons have almost died out now, except in parts of Surrey, and even they tend to be a lot smaller and no longer breathe fire, due to Health and Safety regulations.

In Sir Gadabout's time dragons were as big

as a Tyrannosaurus Rex dinosaur. They were covered in scales as tough as steel, had huge sharp teeth and tails that, with one careless flick, could knock you into outer space.

"Right, there's no sign of Lucky here," said Sir Gadabout after almost one-and-a-half minutes. "We'd better go home for dinner."

"Knights of the Green Cross don't go home for dinner when they're on an important quest," said Sir Mistabit.

"Neither do we," said Sir Gadabout. "I just thought *you* might be hungry."

"Knights of Camelot don't even go home for *tea!*" declared Herbert, and immediately began to wonder if he'd overdone it. He was feeling a little peckish.

Sir Gadabout looked perturbed. "Well, let's not get carried away. We shall see— **DRAGON**!!!" He galloped off at full speed, emitting a strange, high-pitched wail.

The others spun round to see what had alarmed him. The fat hedgehog trundling across the field in front of them didn't *seem* to be breathing fire. By the time they had fetched Sir Gadabout back from several fields away, the hedgehog had gone and they had a

hard job convincing him it had only been a hedgehog.

"It was *enormous*!" he said.

Sir Mistabit was sympathetic for a change. "It *did* come up to a man's knees, I must admit."

"Anyway," added Sir Gadabout, "I wasn't running away. I was investigating dragon footprints. They looked pretty fresh to me."

At first they didn't believe him but it

turned out that he *had* stumbled on dragon tracks.

The footprints in the mud were nearly a metre long, if you included the imprints of the sharp claws.

"Just because it's got big feet, it doesn't mean the dragon itself is all *that* big... does it?" asked Sir Gadabout nervously.

"Big enough to fry *you* up a treat," said Sidney Smith from the safety of Herbert's saddlebag. Being a rather lazy cat, this was how he usually travelled when they were on one of their missions.

Herbert tried to cheer his master up. "I once had a lovely little puppy. *He* had very big feet!"

"Wasn't that the one which grew into the Irish Wolfhound and ate the postman?" asked Sidney Smith.

"Can't remember," replied Herbert defensively.

Sir Gadabout began to feel rather faint. He felt even worse when they found some bones by the side of the track.

"The work of a dragon, definitely," decided Sir Mistabit.

Then they saw scorch marks on some

rocks, and more bones. "We're getting close," the little knight continued expertly (although he had never actually seen a dragon in his life). "I'll soon be running my sword right through him."

"Will you?" cried Sir Gadabout, trying to give a little laugh but sounding more as if he were being throttled. "That's handy, because I think I left the kettle on at home, and I think I'd better—"

Suddenly, they heard a terrifying roar. Smoke was rising from behind a hill ahead of them.

"*My washing!*" Sir Gadabout screamed. "It looks like rain and I've left my socks out and—"

"*CHARGE!*" bellowed Sir Mistabit.

"*Wait!*" yelled Herbert. "We need a plan."

"We need some proper knights, more like," said a voice from inside his saddlebag.

They crept up the hill and peeped over. A dragon the size of a house was chasing a white goat that had a very peculiar way of running owing to having only one front leg and one back leg. Every now and then the dragon whooshed out a long fiery breath and each time the goat just managed to dart out of its way. But it was beginning to tire. It was only a matter of time before the dragon caught up with it.

"*Lucky!*" whispered Sir Mistabit.

"If you say so," murmured Sidney Smith.

"I think you and Sir Mistabit should attack him from different directions, Sire," Herbert

suggested. "That way, at least one of you might
not get . . . er . . . slightly singed."

"We could try throwing stones at it from
here," Sir Gadabout said hopefully. "Very *large*
ones," he added, seeing the scornful looks on
their faces. "Thrown very hard? Oh, all right
then."

Sir Mistabit was already getting back on his

horse. "I'll charge from the east, you charge from the west!"

Within seconds the two knights were circling at high speed, preparing to attack.

But were they too late? The dragon had pounced on the exhausted goat and had her in its razor-sharp claws. The poor creature was bleating so pitifully even Sir Gadabout forgot his fear. He lowered his lance and charged.

Sir Mistabit did the same from the other side.

At first, the dragon didn't notice them. It was too busy lying with Lucky in its grasp, about to enjoy a good meal. But as the thunder of hooves grew louder, he looked up

sharply to see what was happening.

Just as the two knights were about to drive their lances into the huge beast, Sir Mistabit gave his war cry: "**BASH OR BUST!**"

He had a *very* loud voice for such a little man.

"You made me *jump*!" Sir Gadabout cried.

It wasn't a very bright thing to say.

Buck skidded to a halt just millimetres short of the dragon and gave an almighty kick with his back legs. Sir Gadabout sailed through the air and landed on top of the dragon's head.

The dragon leaped to its feet and Sir Mistabit hurtled on under its belly.

Sidney Smith sank back into Herbert's saddlebag with a groan and covered his head with his paws.

"*Heeeelp!*" screeched Sir Gadabout, clinging doggedly to the dragon's ears as it tried to flick him off.

"*Attack!*" bellowed Sir Mistabit, spurring on his horse. But the horse had already had its tail singed by the dragon's fiery breath and was not feeling quite as brave as its master. Instead of charging at the dragon, Sir Mistabit ended up galloping in circles around the creature, shouting and cursing.

The dragon had never seen anything quite like it. Something — he didn't know what — was on his head, making a weird high-pitched noise and pulling painfully on his ears; one horse was jumping up and down, kicking and whinnying, and another was speeding round and round him in circles.

The dragon became so dizzy trying to keep his eyes on everything that was going on that he toppled over and even lying on his back the world still seemed to be spinning very fast.

Sir Gadabout fell off and clattered to the ground.

"*Victory!*" Sir Mistabit cried. "No dragon can withstand the sharp point of my lance!" The small fact that the dragon had never felt the sharp point of his lance hardly seemed

worth quibbling over in the circumstances.

But had they been in time to save Lucky?

While the dragon was still rolling helplessly on its back, Sidney Smith felt brave enough to come out of Herbert's saddlebag. He crept closer to see what had become of the unfortunate mascot.

"Oh, *great*," he sighed, holding up what looked suspiciously like one of Lucky's two

remaining legs. "This is all that's left, thanks to our friends the nutty knights."

"No!" replied Herbert. "I saw Lucky escape!"

"On one leg?" Sidney Smith asked, raising his eyebrows and twitching his whiskers in disbelief.

"Yes!" Herbert insisted. "When the dragon fell over she got away — somehow."

"Then lead the way!" cried Sir Mistabit.

Sir Gadabout picked himself up very carefully and groggily. "Are you sure it's worth it?" he groaned. "After all, there's not much left to rescue."

"*We'll* be the ones who need rescuing before long," Sidney Smith said as he watched

the dragon beginning to recover its senses.
"Let's go!"

As soon as Herbert had calmed Buck down
and Sir Gadabout could get back on him, they
continued with their rescue mission. Surely
Lucky couldn't have got far?

5
The Circus

They headed in the direction Herbert had seen Lucky take, thinking they must easily catch up with her. But very soon they came to a forest and it was impossible to tell which way to go. They searched for hours, without

success, and as darkness fell they had to set up camp for the night deep in the forest.

It was a troubled night. Sir Gadabout had never camped in a forest before, and he was rather worried by the hooting of owls, the howling of wolves, and the strange rustling noises of nocturnal creatures moving about. He dreamt that a dragon had thrown him into a frying pan with some bacon. "*I'm not a sausage!*" he whimpered repeatedly in his sleep, keeping everyone else awake.

Next day they travelled for miles without seeing a soul until late in the afternoon when they emerged from the forest and saw a farmhouse. A little old lady was throwing corn to the chickens in her yard.

"Let's ask her if she's seen Lucky," said Herbert.

"I'd never have thought of that," commented the sarcastic cat.

Sir Gadabout and Sir Mistabit approached the woman. She was small and frail with white hair and a kindly face.

"Good-day, madam," said Sir Gadabout. "I am a knight of—"

"Hello, young man!" the woman said. "You must be worn out. Come in and have a nice cup of tea."

"But we're looking for—"

"I know just how tiring it is when you have to take your children everywhere with you!"

Herbert and Sir Mistabit glowered at her.

"And *cats*!" she continued, spotting Sidney Smith and tweaking his ears rather too hard. "We know what naughty things *they* get up to in the flower beds!"

"I can assure you, madam," said Sidney Smith indignantly, "that I do not, and never have—"

"*Ooh*, I say – almost sounds human, doesn't he? There's a clever puss!" She tweaked his ears again and before they knew it she had marched them all into her farmhouse for a nice cup of tea. The last thing they wanted, while Lucky was still hopping away, was to stop for a nice cup of tea . . . followed by a nice piece of cake . . . followed by some nice home-made scones . . . But as it happened, it turned out to be worth it – *eventually*.

When they finally managed to explain about the goat, she said, "It just so happens I was looking after a stray goat with only one leg, poor thing. But then I found someone who could give her a good home."

"*WHERE*?" cried the four of them together and jumping to their feet.

"Eh? Oh, I think he runs some kind of circus in Lower Downham. *Loves* animals!"

"Thank you very much," Sir Gadabout said. And they hurried out before she could make them another nice cup of tea.

Lower Downham was about ten miles away

but just before getting to the village the would-be goat rescuers came upon a very large red-and-white striped tent. As they came closer they could see jugglers practising, clowns tripping over, and lion tamers taming – the exact kind of thing they had in circuses in Sir Gadabout's day.

"Looks like the circus," said Sir Gadabout.

"Oh? And there I was thinking it was a funeral procession . . ." Sidney Smith remarked.

Sir Mistabit dismounted and asked one of the clowns if he'd seen the goat.

"You'd better ask Signor Fettuccini the ringmaster."

As he was going to find Signor Fettuccini, the clown called back to Sir Mistabit. "Are you any good at falling off horses? We could do with a funny little chap like you in our act—"

"I'm *not* LITTLE!" snapped Sir Mistabit, straightening himself up as much as possible.

Sidney Smith sauntered over to the clown. "Forget it. You're out of your league, mate. We've got the best two clowns in the business here."

Signor Fettuccini was busy painting some kind of sign or poster. Herbert was detailed to talk to him. Neither he nor any of the others could speak Italian but at least Herbert owned an atlas.

"BONJOUR," shouted Herbert in a very loud voice, hoping it might help. "WE ARE LOOKING FOR A GOAT." He made a bleating noise that was supposed to sound like a goat but actually sounded more like a hungry guinea pig.

"THE GOAT IS A *WHITE* GOAT. SEE..."
said Herbert, pulling out the elasticated waist-
band of his underpants – the only white thing
he could find.

Signor Fettuccini was an elderly gentleman
wearing a very impressive purple cloak and
matching felt hat. As he watched Herbert
making noises like a guinea pig and pulling at
his underpants, his eyes began to swivel
around wildly, as if looking for an escape route

or possibly a big stick with which to defend himself.

"THE GOAT IS NOT ALL THERE."

Herbert lifted one of his legs in the air and kept patting it with the hand that wasn't holding his underpants. "NOT ONE AT EACH CORNER – *NO* – BUT ONLY ONE – SEE?"

Sidney Smith groaned. "Even I can't make him out, and I *know* what he's trying to say."

"I think it's rather good," said Sir Gadabout.

"You speak his language," the cat pointed out.

"What *is* he on about?" asked Signor Fettuccini in a decidedly English accent.

"We... we thought you were Italian," mumbled Sir Gadabout.

"What for?"

"Never mind," interjected Sir Mistabit. "Have you seen a stray goat lately?"

"No, I haven't." They noticed him trying to cover up the sign he had been painting.

"Thank you, my man. We bid you good day," said Sir Gadabout.

But Sidney Smith had nipped under Signor Fettucini's legs to get a good look at the poster he had been painting. "It says *Guiseppe and his Amazing Hopping Goat*!" the cat declared.

"It isn't a *real* goat," laughed Signor Fettuccini. "It's a . . . a poodle."

"With one leg?" asked Sidney Smith, studying the picture on the sign.

"Ooh, no – that's just my bad painting," the ringmaster assured him. "I'm not very good at legs, so I decided just to do the one."

At that moment, a man with an enormous belly sauntered along. "Got her to jump through a hoop, boss!" he cried excitedly. And hopping right behind him was Lucky!

"Get the goat!" roared Sir Mistabit.

Signor Fettuccini pushed Sir Mistabit over and ran. "Quick, Bill – don't let them get it!" The pair of them ran into the Big Top – the gigantic tent where the circus was held – with Sir Gadabout and the others in hot pursuit. They soon had the two men and the goat surrounded. Lucky, having finally noticed her long-lost master, was bleating to join him but was tightly held on a piece of rope.

"You might as well hand her over," Sir Mistabit said firmly. "You can't get away from us now."

"Oh, can't they?" growled a deep voice. Coming up behind them was the circus strongman, a gigantic, muscular fellow

covered in tattoos.

Sir Gadabout strode to meet him. "Now look here, I am a Knight of the Round Table—"

"Oh – *round*, is it?" The strongman picked Sir Gadabout up off the ground and proceeded to crumple him up in his armour like some people crush drinks cans. "Well, now *you're* round, too!" And he bowled Sir Gadabout at his comrades and knocked them over like skittles.

Sir Mistabit sprang to his feet and made a dash for Lucky. He was too nippy for the strongman but a flying figure suddenly sent him sprawling. A trapeze artist had leapt from one of the high swings and landed right on top of the miniature knight.

"*Retreat!*" Sir Gadabout cried dizzily from inside his ball of armour as it spun round and round on the sawdust floor.

Sir Mistabit had been pretty well squashed by the blow from above and was now only about half his previous height. It looked as though they had been defeated, and poor Lucky was bleating sadly.

But then, Signor Fettuccini pointed to one of the trapeze swings way up in the roof of

the Big Top. "What on earth is that?"

There was a shriek of "*BANZAI*!" and a turtle wearing a quite snazzy leotard launched itself like a guided missile.

CRACK! He caught the strongman on the head like a coconut at a fair.

BUMP, BANG, WHACK! He bounced from one head to another like a stone skimming across the water until all the baddies were lying on the ground groaning.

The turtle punched the air triumphantly.

"*YES!*"

"Dr McPherson!" cried Sidney Smith in admiration. "You finally got it right!"

(They later discovered that the rabbit Dr McPherson had been riding had a cousin in Lower Downham.)

When they arrived back at Camelot they caused quite a stir. Sir Mistabit was about the size of a milk carton and waddled along like an accordion on legs. Sir Gadabout was rolled home by Herbert, with Sidney Smith pestering him to see if Sir Gadabout would bounce.

But ever since the cat had kicked the ball of armour that was Sir Gadabout between two trees and shouted "*GOAL!*", Herbert had totally ignored him.

Sir Melville, in charge of the Knights of the Green Cross, was slightly disappointed that rather less of his goat had come back than had

set off, but he soon cheered up when Guinevere knocked up three very stylish wooden
legs for Lucky.

There was still the small matter of the
contest between Sir Mistabit and Sir Gadabout. It was a *very* close run thing. Everyone
knew deep down that Sir Gadabout was still

the Worst Knight in the World but they were so thankful to get Lucky back it was quite a while before they mentioned it again.